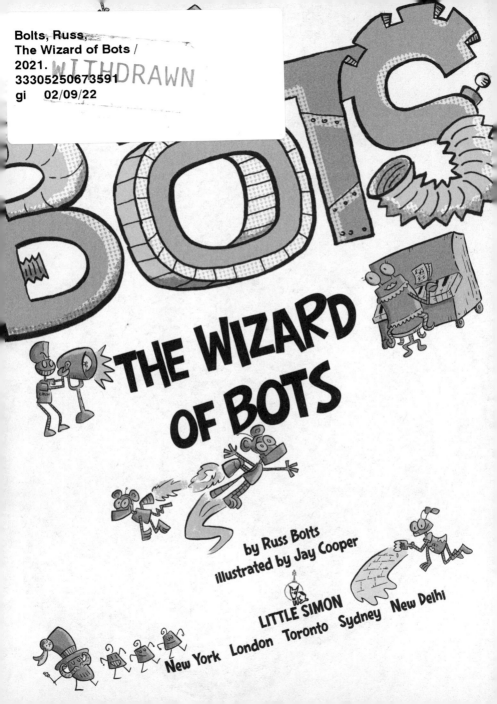

BOTS

THE WIZARD OF BOTS

by Russ Bolts
illustrated by Jay Cooper

LITTLE SIMON

New York   London   Toronto   Sydney   New Delhi

LITTLE SIMON
An imprint of Simon & Schuster Children's Publishing Division • 1230 Avenue of the Americas, New York, New York 10020 • First Little Simon hardcover edition April 2021 • Copyright © 2021 by Simon & Schuster, Inc. Also available in a Little Simon paperback edition All rights reserved, including the right of reproduction in whole or in part in any form. LITTLE SIMON is a registered trademark of Simon & Schuster, Inc., and associated colophon is a trademark of Simon & Schuster, Inc. For information about special discounts for bulk purchases, please contact Simon & Schuster Special Sales at 1-866-506-1949 or business@simonandschuster.com. The Simon & Schuster Speakers Bureau can bring authors to your live event. For more information or to book an event contact the Simon & Schuster Speakers Bureau at 1-866-248-3049 or visit our website at www.simonspeakers.com. Manufactured in the United States of America 0221 FFG

2 4 6 8 10 9 7 5 3 1

Cataloging-in-Publication Data is available for this title from the Library of Congress.

ISBN 978-1-5344-8639-3 (pbk)
ISBN 978-1-5344-8640-9 (hc)
ISBN 978-1-5344-8641-6 (eBook)

CONTENTS

CHAPTER 1

Acting!

DARKNESS.
IN THIS MOMENT,
ANYTHING IS
POSSIBLE.

YOU MAY REMEMBER ME FROM SUCH PLAYS AND FILMS AS:
A BOT'S CAR NAMED D3SIR3, A BOT'S HOUSE, BOT ON A HOT TIN ROOF, THE BOTTENING!, THE PRINCESS BOT, AND, OF COURSE, WHO COULD FORGET ABOUT ROBO-MOM.
A BOT'S CAR NAMED D3SIR3
D3SIR3
SMELLA!
A Bot's House

15

20

23

26

44

47

58

Wicked Tinny

63

75

77

83

85

87

89

90

93

BIG BATTLE DAY

- Put water in large pot
  - Boil
  - Toil
  - Trouble
    - Feed cat
    - Clean litter box
- Gather spells at the spell store
  - Buy more warts
  - Need newt eyes
- Dust the castle with more dust
- Add spiderwebs to every corner
  - Get Dorothy
  - And her little dog, too
    - A present

100